Usborne **ART** ideas

Making cards

Fiona Watt

Designed and illustrated by
Non Figg and Antonia Miller

Additional illustrations by Abigail Brown,
Katrina Fearn and Samantha Meredith

Photographs by Howard Allman
Cover designed by Josephine Thompson

Contents

4 Materials
6 Different papers

Card designs

8 Swirly flowers
10 Stylish shoes
12 Stand-up animals

14 Birthday cakes
16 Pop-up buildings
18 Black and white animals
20 Rocket launch
22 Silver swirls
24 Textured birds
26 Ink bugs
28 Decorated drawings
30 Striped patterns

32 Wrapping paper kites
34 Stitched flowers
36 Fold-out cards
38 Glittery patterns
40 Watercolour leaves
42 Embossed shapes
44 Zigzag rocketeers
46 Patchwork paper
48 Printed animals

50 Dry brush flowers
52 Folded tissue paper
54 Handbags
56 Zigzag clowns
58 Collage animals

60 Making envelopes
62 Other ideas
64 Index

Materials

The ideas in this book use a variety of materials which can be found in art or craft shops and most stationers. Turn to pages 6-7 to find out about different papers and how to add patterns and textures to them.

Crayons

Paintbrush

Dip pen

Coloured pencils

Felt-tip pens

Paints, inks and pens

Different pens, pencils, paints and inks are used to make the cards in this book. If you don't have a dip pen and bottled ink, use a cartridge pen or a thin black felt-tip pen, instead.

Ink

The shoe card below was made using watercolour paints, coloured pencils and a black felt-tip pen.

Watercolour paints

Using a craft knife

Some of the projects suggest using a craft knife to cut out shapes. When you use one, always put an old magazine or a piece of thick cardboard under the paper you are cutting. Be very careful of the sharp blade, too.

Scraps of paper for collage.

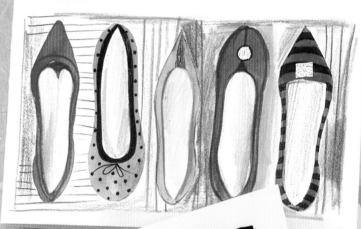

Use thick coloured paper to make your cards.

This clown card was made with patterned paper ripped from old magazines.

Use a safety craft knife like this one, but keep your fingers away from the blade.

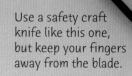

Glitter

Glitter glue pens   Metallic pens

Parcel ribbon

This hat card was made with a dip pen, ink and a ribbon.

Envelopes

Find out on pages 60-61 how to make your own envelopes. If you're going to use a bought envelope, cut your card to fit the envelope before you start.

Material and threads

The flower cards on pages 34-35 and the collage animals on 58-59 are made using scraps of material and have a little stitching on them, as well as buttons, beads and sequins.

Thick thread

Beads and sequins

Different kinds of material

Material, glue, thread, buttons and ribbons were used on this cat card.

Ribbon

Scissors

Different papers

The cards in this book are made with different kinds of paper. Under each heading you will find a suggestion for the type of paper to use. Several of the cards use textured papers – find out on the opposite page how to make them.

Thick paper or thin cardboard is best to make the actual card.

This flower card has been made with thin cardboard.

Coloured paper

Find out on pages 24-25 how to make birds like these from textured papers.

You can use thick cartridge paper instead of thin cardboard to make a card.

These swirly patterns are painted with watercolours on watercolour paper.

Sponged paper

Dry brushed paper

Spattered paint

Wrapping paper

You can use wrapping paper as well as paper ripped from old magazines.

Sponging

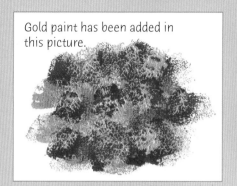

Gold paint has been added in this picture.

1. Dip a piece of sponge into some paint, then dab it onto a piece of paper. Dip it into the paint each time you dab it on the paper.

2. When the paint is dry, lightly dab a darker shade of paint over the top, but leave some of the original colour showing through.

You can even dab a third colour of paint on top, leaving some of the other colours showing through, like this.

Dry brushing

1. Dip a thick, dry paintbrush into thick paint, so that the paint just coats the tips of the bristles. Use acrylic paint if you have it.

2. Brush the paint around and around in a circle on a piece of paper, pressing hard so that you make lots of individual brushmarks.

Instead of dry brushing a circle, try brushing lines across the paper, so that you see the brushmarks. Brush another colour on top.

Spattering paint

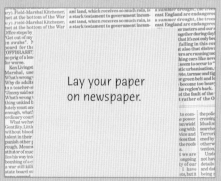

Lay your paper on newspaper.

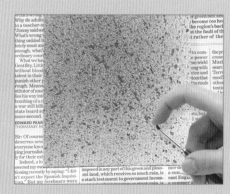

1. Spattering paint can be very messy, so do this outside. Pour some paint into a container, then mix in a little water to make it runny.

2. Dip an old toothbrush into the paint. Pull a fingernail along the bristles, <u>towards</u> you, to spatter the paint. Do it until you cover the paper.

To get bigger spatters, dip a paintbrush into runny paint. Holding the brush over the paper, run a finger over the bristles, towards you, like this.

Swirly flowers

THIN CARDBOARD

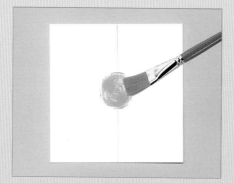

1. Cut a square of thin cardboard. Then, pressing very lightly, draw a faint pencil line down the middle of the cardboard.

2. Dip the tip of the bristles of a thick, dry brush into orange paint. Then, brush around and around to make a flower in the middle of the square.

3. Brush two more flowers above and below the first one, overlapping the pencil line just a little. Paint green stems and leaves, too.

Don't cut through the card.

4. When the paint is dry, use a dark orange pencil to draw a spiral in each flower. Draw around the leaves with a green pencil and add veins.

5. Then, lay a ruler along the pencil line. Gently run a craft knife along the line to score it, but don't score through the flowers.

Use scissors to cut around the leaves and flowers.

6. Use the craft knife to cut around the flowers on the left-hand side of the pencil line, only. (Where to cut is shown here in blue.)

7. Gently fold the card along the scored line. Then, cut around the leaves, stalk and flowers on the right-hand side of the card.

Try different shapes of
flowers, such as tulips,
as well as swirly circles.

The card on the right
has the fold along
the top rather than
down the side.

9

Stylish shoes

THICK PAPER, WATERCOLOUR PAINT AND COLOURED PENCILS

Leave some unpainted gaps.

1. Fold a piece of thick white paper in half to make a card. Then, paint blocks of colour on the front with watery watercolour paints.

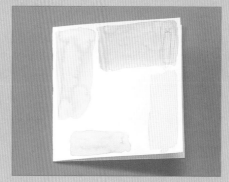

2. When the paint is dry, use a pencil to draw a shoe inside one of the blocks of paint. Draw it as if you were looking at the shoe from above.

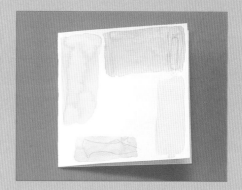

3. Then, draw another elegant shoe in a different block of paint, but this time draw it as if you were looking at it side-on.

4. Fill the card with lots more different kinds of shoes, such as boots and sandals, as well as some men's shoes. Add patterns and laces, too.

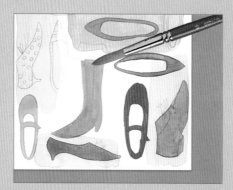

5. Fill in the shoes with watercolour paints or felt-tip pens. Leave some shoes unpainted, letting the blocks of colour show through.

6. Then, use a black pen to decorate the shoes and fill in some parts of them. Add spots, stripes, bows and buckles to some of them, too.

7. Use coloured pencils to add shading to some of the shoes. Roughly shade inside some shoes, and add shading in the spaces between them.

8. For a shiny buckle, cut a little square from some foil. Fold it in half and cut a rectangle from the fold. Open it out and glue it on the boot.

9. Use coloured pencils to draw some thick lines to fill in any gaps on the card. Make the lines go in different directions.

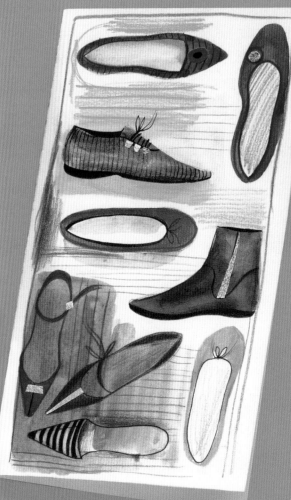
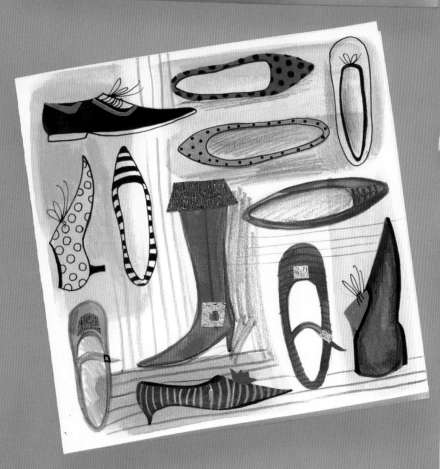
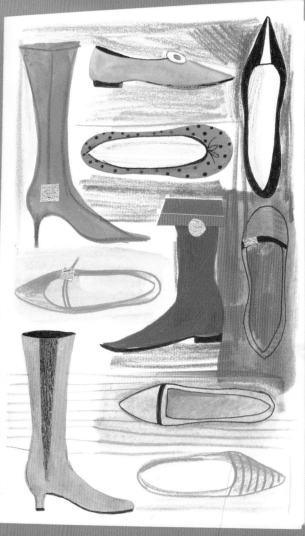

Stand-up animals

COLOURED PAPER

For a bird, cut two large circles for the eyes and glue them onto the front of the card.

See 'Other ideas' for how to make the sheep's body a different colour to its head.

Glue on big ears and draw on a nose for a dog card.

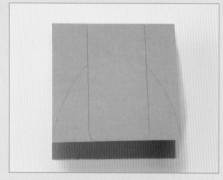

1. To make a crocodile card, fold a piece of thick green paper in half. Draw a long head, then add 'shoulders' on either side of it.

2. Keeping the paper folded, cut around the head and body, but don't cut along the fold across the top of the crocodile's head.

3. Then, cut along the pencil lines at the sides of the head, cutting through the top layer of the card only. Open the card and stand it up.

Write your message inside the card, but be careful not to let it show when the card stands up.

Cut out a tuft of hair and glue it on for a horse's mane.

The spots on this cow were glued on.

Other ideas

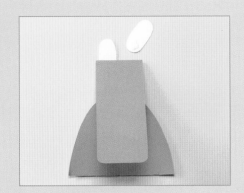

You could add shapes inside, too.

4. Draw two ovals for eyes on white paper. Cut them out and glue them onto the back of the head. Draw pupils in the eyes and add nostrils.

To make the body a different colour to the animal's face, glue another piece of paper inside the folded card before you draw on the front.

For a coloured beak lay a piece of coloured paper under the head and draw around it. Cut out the shape and glue it onto the head.

Birthday cakes

THICK PAPER OR THIN CARDBOARD

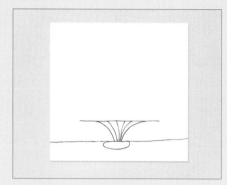

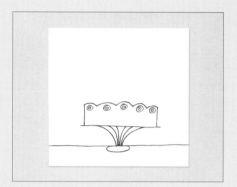

1. Fold a rectangle of thick paper or thin cardboard in half to make a card. Use a very thin black felt-tip pen to draw a line across the bottom.

2. Draw an oval below the line for the base of a cake stand. Then, draw a line for the stand, and curved lines joining it to the base.

3. Draw the bottom layer of the cake, making the top edge of it bumpy. Then, add a little spiral inside each of the bumps.

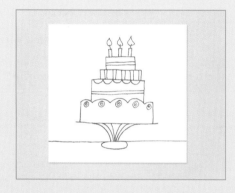

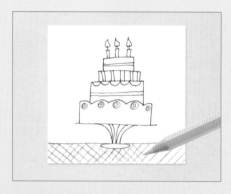

4. Draw three more layers on top of the cake. Then, add patterns of lines and spots inside each layer. Draw three candles on top of the cake.

5. For a tablecloth, draw diagonal lines one way, then the other, so that they crisscross. Don't fill in the base of the cake stand.

6. Fill in the bottom layer of the cake with a chalk pastel. Smudge it a little with your finger. Then, fill in the layers above with coloured pencils.

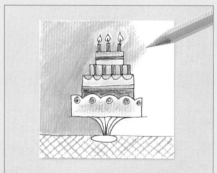

7. Fill in the candles, but leave the flames white. Draw a yellow halo around the flames, then go over it with orange. Finally, fill in the background.

Use the ideas here to draw different types of cakes on your cards.

Pop-up buildings

THICK PAPER AND FELT-TIP PENS

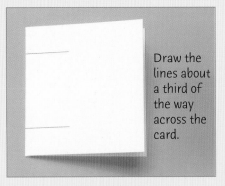

Draw the lines about a third of the way across the card.

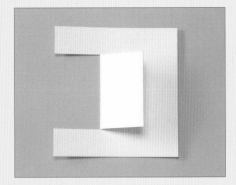

1. Cut two rectangles the same size from thick paper and fold them both in half. Put one of them to one side to use for the back of the card in step 9.

2. Draw a straight line coming in from the fold, a little way from the top of the paper. Draw another line, the same length, at the bottom.

3. Keeping the paper folded, cut along the lines to make a flap. Fold the flap to the front and then to the back, creasing the fold well each time.

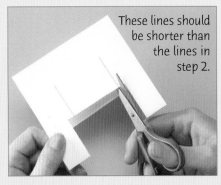

These lines should be shorter than the lines in step 2.

Hold the big flap as you push the second one through.

4. Open the card and push the flap through to the inside of the card, like this. Then, carefully close the card and smooth it flat.

5. Draw two more lines a little way in from the corners of the flap. Open the card a little and push a scissor blade inside the flap, like this.

6. Cut along the lines to make a second flap. Fold the flap to the front and crease the fold. Then, open the card and push the second flap through.

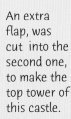

An extra flap, was cut into the second one, to make the top tower of this castle.

These two cards had little flaps cut along the folded edge of the large flap.

7. Open the card flat. Then, draw the trees and sky with felt-tip pens above the middle fold. Add ground below it, but don't draw over the flaps.

8. Draw windows and a door on the flaps to look like the front of a house. Then, cut a roof from thick paper, fill it in and glue it onto the top flap.

Don't glue the flaps.

9. Fold the card up again so that so that the flaps become 3-D. Then, glue the house onto the folded card from step 1, matching the folds.

The skyscraper below had an extra flap cut into it, too. The gorilla's feet and hand were drawn onto the flaps, while the rest of its body is on the background.

Black and white animals

THIN BLACK PEN

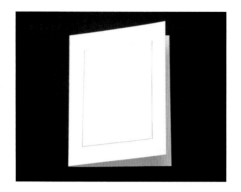

1. Fold a piece of thin white cardboard in half to make a card. Then, draw a rectangle in the middle of the card, using a pencil and a ruler.

2. Slip a piece of thick cardboard inside the card. Then, carefully cut out the rectangle with a craft knife, to make a 'window'.

3. Use a thin black felt-tip pen to draw around the window. Then, draw a slightly smaller rectangle to make a frame. Open the card.

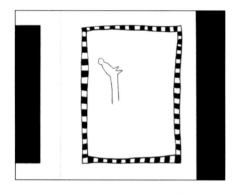

4. Draw stripes inside the frame and fill them in. Draw two lines for a zebra's neck inside the frame. Add two pointed ears and a nose.

5. Draw a rectangular body, then add the legs and a wispy tail. Add dots for the eyes and nostrils, then draw stripes all over the zebra.

6. Draw a line above the zebra, then add a sun and some clouds above it. Draw a line for the ground and add some tufts of grass.

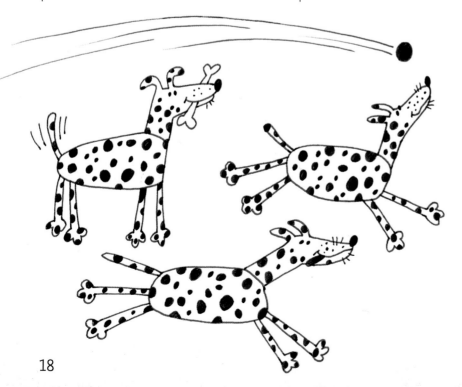

7. Open the card and lay it flat so you can see the front of the card. Draw a frame around the window, then decorate it with dots.

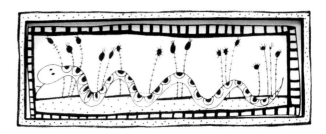

You can make the window any shape you like, so long as you can think of an animal that will fit inside it!

Write your message inside the card, around the edge of the picture.

Rocket launch

THICK PAPER AND FELT-TIP PENS

Crease the folds well.

1. Cut a long strip from thick paper and fold it in half. Fold over the paper again, so that the folded edge is about a third of the way up the paper.

You should see the paper underneath here.

2. Turn the paper over. Then, fold down the top of the paper, so that part of the paper from underneath is showing along the top.

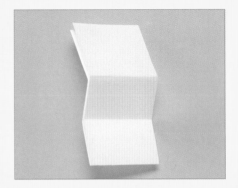

3. Unfold the strip, so that it is only folded in half. Then, turn the paper around so that fold is at the bottom of the strip.

4. Draw a straight line down the paper, a little way in from one side. Then, draw another line the same distance in from the opposite side.

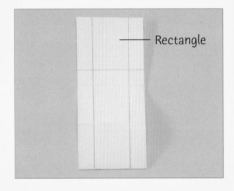

Rectangle

5. Draw a straight line across the paper, a little way above the top fold, to make a rectangle in the middle of the top section.

Draw the 'whoosh' as far as the pencil line.

6. Draw a rocket in a top corner of the rectangle. Add a 'whoosh' below it and some clouds around it. Go over the lines with a black pen.

These three photographs show how the rocket pops up.

7. Fill in your drawing using felt-tip pens. Then, holding the layers together, cut around the outline, but don't cut below the pencil line.

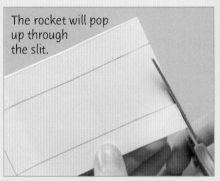

The rocket will pop up through the slit.

8. Make a slit in the middle fold by cutting away a small piece of paper between the pencil lines. Then, unfold the strip of paper.

The bottom of this fairy card is decorated shiny stickers.

All these cards were made in exactly the same way as the rocket card.

The cards will fold completely flat to fit inside an envelope.

Use a silver pen to draw dots for stars.

9. Fold the paper in half again so that the rocket is hidden inside. Then, fill in the bottom section on each side, to look like the sky in space.

10. Unfold the strip again and crease all the folds towards the middle fold. Then, fold the sections with the rocket shapes into the middle.

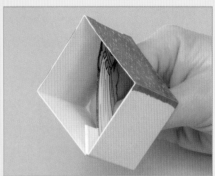

11. Spread glue on back of the rocket section. Then, press the two end sections together, matching the edges. Let the glue dry.

Silver swirls

FOIL, SILVER PEN AND THICK PAPER

Spread the glue on the dull side of the foil.

1. Fold a rectangle of thick red paper in half to make a card. Cut out a square of silver foil and glue it at an angle onto the card.

2. Cut a small rectangle from a piece of red paper. Fold it in half, then draw half a heart against the fold. Cut out the shape you have drawn.

3. Open out the paper with the heart cut out of it and run a fingernail over the fold to flatten it. Then, glue the paper in the middle of the foil.

4. Starting at one corner, use a silver pen to draw swirly spirals on the foil. Draw the spirals so that they curl around each other.

Experiment with different patterns drawn on the foil.

Make a rectangular card with three foil squares glued on.

Other ideas

You could draw a thick spiral in silver pen on the shiny side of a foil square. Then, draw thinner spirals around it to fill the square.

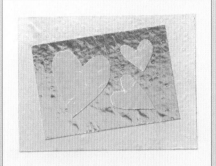

Cut out hearts from foil, then glue them dull-side up onto a foil rectangle. Then, glue the rectangle onto the dull side of another piece of foil.

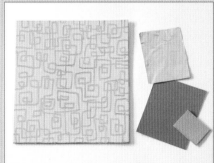

Instead of drawing swirling spirals, use a silver pen to draw a continuous pattern of straight lines. Glue coloured paper and foil squares on top.

23

Textured birds

TEXTURED PAPERS

1. Texture several pieces of paper using different colours and techniques, from page 7. Then, leave the pieces of paper to dry.

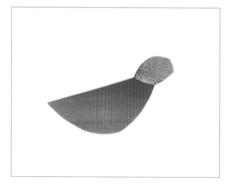

2. Cut a shape for a bird's body from one of the papers. Cut a shape for the head from another piece of paper and glue it onto the body.

3. Draw a dot for an eye, then cut out a beak and glue it on. Cut out a shape for a crest, then cut thin triangles out of one edge of it.

This tall bird
had an extra
strip of paper
added for a
long neck.

This blue bird had one of
the wings glued onto the
back of the body.

Use the ideas shown here
to make a bird to glue
onto the front of a card.

4. Glue the crest onto the
back of the head. Then, make
a shape for some tail feathers
and glue them onto the front
of the body.

5. Cut out a shape for the
wing and glue it onto the
body. Then, cut some thin
strips of paper and glue them
onto the wing.

6. Cut strips for the legs and
glue them on. Then, cut out
the feet and cut triangles into
one side of them, for toes.
Glue the feet onto the legs.

Ink bugs

PENCILS, INK PEN AND THICK PAPER

Draw the shapes at different angles.

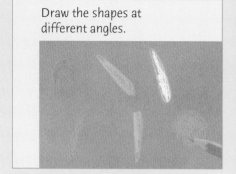

1. Fold a rectangle of thick paper in half to make a card. Then, draw simple shapes for bugs' bodies all over the card with coloured pencils.

Add a second colour to some of the wings, too.

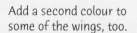

2. Use a different colour of pencil to draw spots, stripes, and shading along the bodies. Then, add wings to some of the bugs, too.

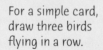

3. Use a dip pen or fountain pen to draw around the shapes – you don't need to stick to the shapes exactly. Add ink dots and spots, too.

A dip pen will give you slightly uneven lines, like the lines on all the cards shown here.

For a simple card, draw three birds flying in a row.

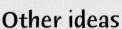

Other ideas

For a fishy card, draw simple fish shapes with coloured pencils on blue paper. Add fins, then go over the outlines with a blue ink pen.

Pale shades of coloured pencils, like the white, pink and blue above, show up better on darker paper than deep colours.

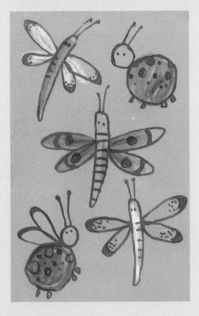

For a bird card, draw simple bodies at different angles on the card. Add wings, then outline the shapes and draw spots and feathers.

You could make little cards, like the ones above and below, as gift tags.

For a flowery card, draw flowers with pencils, then outline the shapes. Fill in the spaces between the flowers with seed pods and spirals.

Decorated drawings

INK PEN, BEADS AND RIBBON

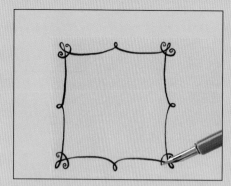

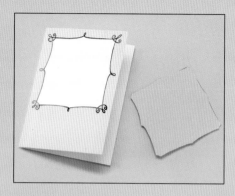

1. Fold a piece of thin white cardboard in half to make a card. Then, draw around it on a piece of coloured paper and cut out the shape.

2. Draw a fancy, curly frame at the top of the paper. Then, use a black ink pen or felt-tip pen to draw over all the pencil lines. Let the ink dry.

3. Lay the paper on an old magazine, then carefully cut out the middle of the frame with a craft knife. Glue the frame onto the card.

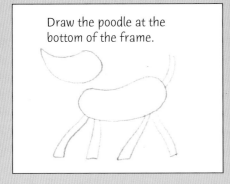

4. Use a pencil to draw a sausage shape for a poodle's body. Draw a head, shaped like a tear, and two lines for the tail. Add legs, too.

5. Draw curly fur on its head and its bottom. Add some fur on each leg and at the tip of its tail. Then, erase the pencil lines inside the patches of fur.

6. Draw a hand with a long wrist and the cuff of a coat in the top corner of the frame. Then, draw a diagonal line for a lead.

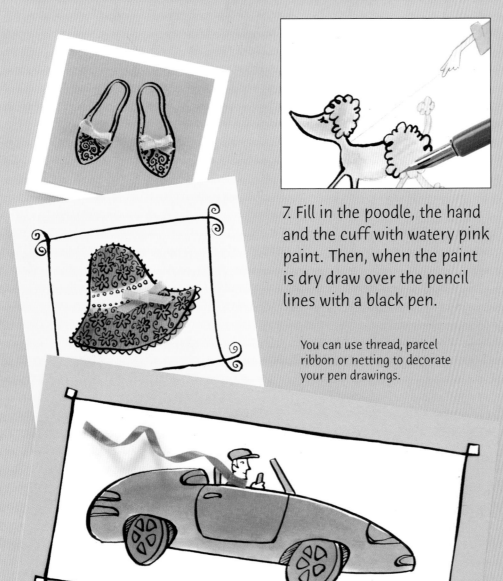

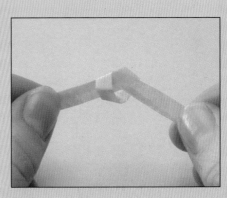

7. Fill in the poodle, the hand and the cuff with watery pink paint. Then, when the paint is dry draw over the pencil lines with a black pen.

You can use thread, parcel ribbon or netting to decorate your pen drawings.

8. Spread a line of white glue on the poodle's neck, then press two rows of little beads onto the glue, for a collar. Add a bracelet on the wrist, too.

9. For a bow, cut a thin strip of tissue paper and fold it in half. Tie a knot in the paper, then cut off the ends to make a bow. Glue it onto the head.

Striped patterns

COLOURED PAPER

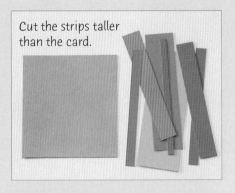

Cut the strips taller than the card.

1. Cut a piece of thick blue paper the size that you want your card to be. Then, cut strips of different widths from brightly coloured papers.

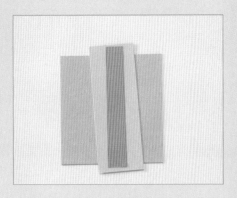

2. Glue one strip across the blue paper at an angle, letting it overlap the top and bottom edges. Then, glue another strip on top of it.

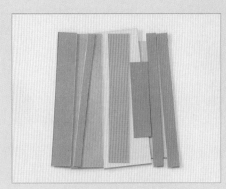

3. Glue on more strips at different angles, making them overlap. Glue some thinner strips completely on top of others, too.

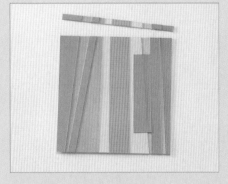

4. Then, turn the blue paper over and cut off the ends of all the strips which are overlapping the top and bottom edges.

Add other simple geometric shapes, such as squares and rectangles, as well as half-circles.

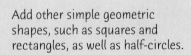

5. Lay a ruler along the top of the paper and use a craft knife to trim off a thin strip. Glue this strip on top of the other strips.

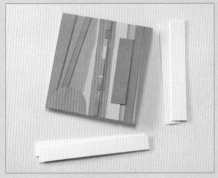

6. Cut a half circle from a piece of paper and glue it on. Then, glue your decorated paper onto a folded card and trim the edges to fit.

Wrapping paper kites

WRAPPING PAPER AND THICK PAPER

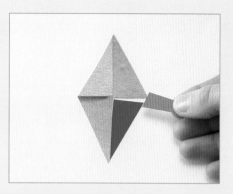

1. Paint a rectangle of thick paper to give it a textured effect (see page 7). When the paint is dry, fold the paper in half to make a card.

2. Draw a triangle on a piece of wrapping paper and cut it out. Then, cut out three more triangles, the same size, from different wrapping papers.

3. Arrange the triangles in a kite shape and glue them onto a piece of thick paper. If there are any gaps glue a little paper shape on top.

Try making balloons, or airships, too.

4. Cut out the kite and glue it onto the card. Make more kites and glue them on, too. Trim off any parts of the kites which overlap the edges.

5. Then, cut out lots of little triangles from different wrapping papers and glue one on the top and sides of each kite.

6. For the kites' tails, glue lots of little triangles curving down in a line. Glue them on so that they overlap each other a little.

You could make a Valentine's card with heart-shaped kites, like the one below.

These cards
would make
lovely birthday,
Easter or
Mother's Day
cards.

Stitched flowers

SCRAPS OF MATERIAL, THICK PAPER AND BEADS

1. Fold a square of thick paper in half to make a card. Cut two squares of material that will fit one above the other on the card.

Pull the threads gently.

2. To make frayed edges around one of the squares, gradually pull the threads away from the edges, one at a time.

3. Cut two smaller squares from patterned material. Glue the smaller squares in the middle of the larger ones, then let the glue dry.

4. Meanwhile, cut out two flower shapes and two small circles for the middles from different materials. Glue the shapes onto the squares.

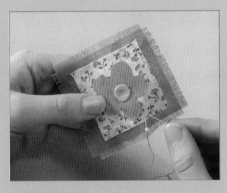

5. When all the glue is dry, sew little beads all around the edge of one of the squares. Secure the end of the thread with little stitches.

6. Stitch three long stitches, crossing each other in the middle of the other flower. Then, glue both squares onto the card.

7. Thread a needle and tie a knot in the end. Push the needle up from the back, through the card, and out into the corner of the top square.

8. Stitch in and out all the way around the square with running stitches. Then, secure the thread at the back with a piece of sticky tape.

9. Stitch around the other square with cross stitches (two diagonal stitches that cross each other). Secure the end of the thread at the back.

Fold-out cards

THICK PAPER

Fill in the map with paints and pencils.

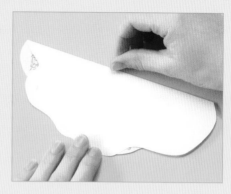

1. For a pirate card, draw a treasure map on a piece of thick paper and fill it in. When the paint is dry cut a wavy shape around it.

2. Fold the map in half so that the picture is on the inside. Then, lay it on a flat surface and run a fingernail along the fold to crease it well.

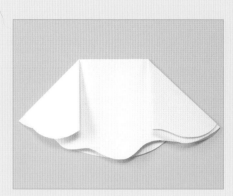

3. Fold over both ends of the map, like this, and crease the folds well. Then, turn the map over and crease the same folds again.

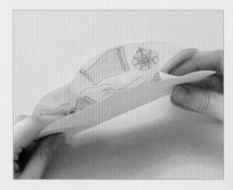

4. Open the map and push in one end along the folds. Then, fold in the other end in the same way. Close the map and crease all the folds.

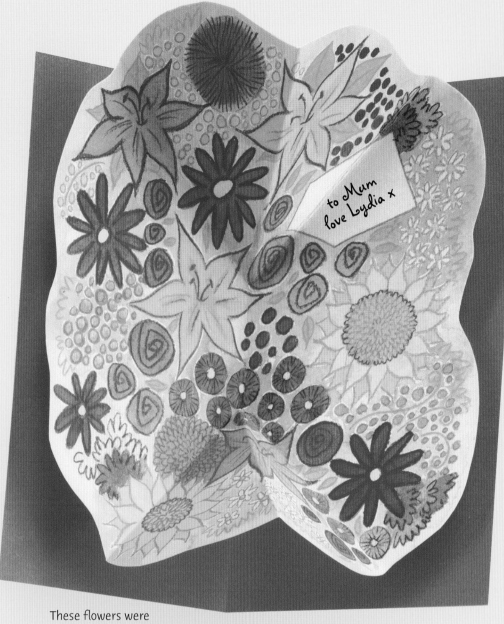

to Mum
love Lydia x

These flowers were painted, then decorated with coloured pencils.

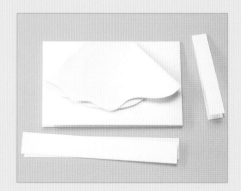

5. To make the card, fold a piece of thick paper in half and lay the map on top. Trim the card so that the map will lie inside when it is folded.

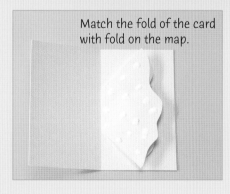

Match the fold of the card with fold on the map.

6. Spread glue on one side of the folded map. Put it inside the card, matching the folds. Glue the top of the map and press on the front of the card.

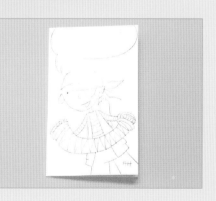

7. Draw a pirate on the front of the card. Fill in the picture with paints and let them dry. Then, go over all the lines with a coloured pencil.

Glittery patterns

GLITTER GLUE AND TEXTURED PAPER

The white paper should be about the size of your card.

1. Fold a piece of thick paper in half to make a card. Then, use glitter glue to draw swirly shapes all over a piece of white paper. Let the glue dry.

You could make a card, like the one above, which is folded along the top rather than down the side.

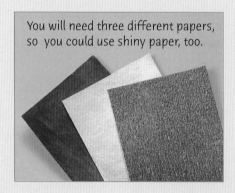

You will need three different papers, so you could use shiny paper, too.

2. While the glue is drying, make textured papers by sponging and dry brushing paint onto coloured paper (see page 7).

3. When the paint is dry, cut a strip from the swirly gold paper and glue it across the middle of the card. Trim off the ends to fit.

4. Cut two strips from one of the textured papers. Glue them on the top and bottom of the card. Glue another strip across the middle.

5. Cut two strips of shiny paper and glue them on, slightly overlapping the textured strips at the top and bottom of the card.

6. Glue another shiny strip across the middle of the card. Then, cut out little squares from one of the textured papers and glue them on.

You could make glittery wrapping paper to match your card.

Watercolour leaves

THICK PAPER AND WATERCOLOUR PAINTS

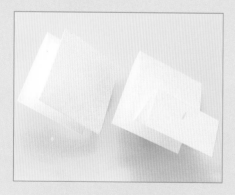

1. Cut a long, rectangular piece of thin cardboard. Fold it into three equal sections. Then, fold the front section in half, like this.

2. Mix some orange watercolour paint with water, then paint a curved shape along the bottom of the front section, for the ground.

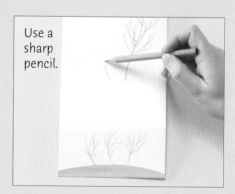

Use a sharp pencil.

3. Draw wavy lines for branches on the front and middle sections of the card. Draw little lines, coming out from the main branches, too.

You can also paint the branches on a simple folded card.

Try drawing branches drooping down from the top of a card.

You could use unrealistic shades of paints, like these pinks and purples, to fill in the leaves.

4. Draw a slightly thicker pencil line at the base of the branches. Then, draw tiny leaves at the ends of a few of the thin branches.

5. Use dark green watercolour paint to paint simple leaf shapes on some of the branches. Leave the paint to dry.

Overlap some of the leaves.

6. Paint more leaves with lighter green paint. When the paint is dry, add more leaves with orange and yellow paints.

Embossed shapes

THICK CARTRIDGE OR WATERCOLOUR PAPER

Heart card

1. Draw a small heart on a piece of cardboard and cut it out. Glue the heart onto another piece of cardboard and let the glue dry.

2. Lay thick paper over the cardboard heart. Rub around the edge of the heart with the end of a paintbrush until you see the embossed shape.

You could overlap some of the painted hearts.

3. Rub over the heart more times in different places on the paper. Then, paint little hearts in the spaces between the embossed shapes.

Snowflake card

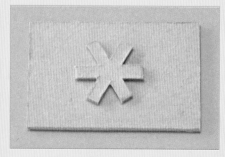

1. For snowflakes, draw a simple snowflake on a piece of cardboard. Cut it out with a craft knife and glue it onto a piece of cardboard.

2. Mix watery green, blue and lilac paint. Then, paint some rough squares on a small piece of thick paper. Let the paint dry.

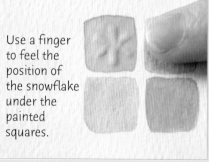

Use a finger to feel the position of the snowflake under the painted squares.

3. Lay one of the painted squares over the cardboard snowflake. Rub around the edges, then move the paper and emboss the shape again.

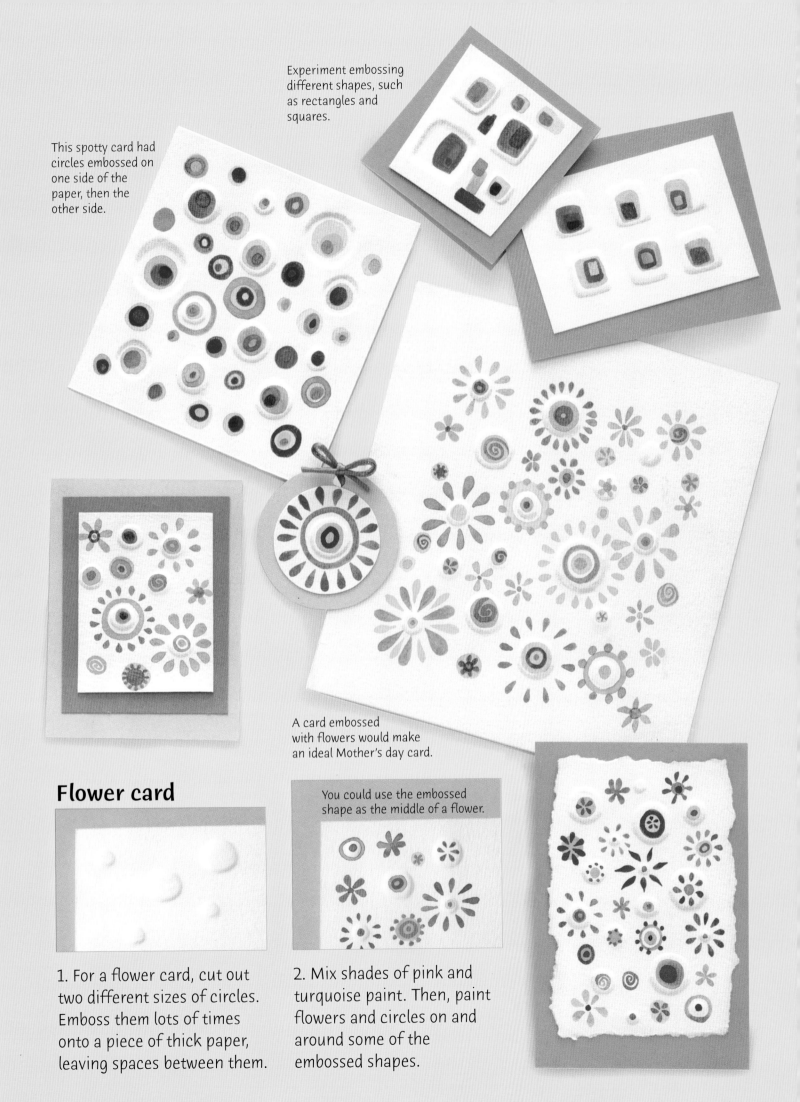

Experiment embossing different shapes, such as rectangles and squares.

This spotty card had circles embossed on one side of the paper, then the other side.

A card embossed with flowers would make an ideal Mother's day card.

Flower card

You could use the embossed shape as the middle of a flower.

1. For a flower card, cut out two different sizes of circles. Emboss them lots of times onto a piece of thick paper, leaving spaces between them.

2. Mix shades of pink and turquoise paint. Then, paint flowers and circles on and around some of the embossed shapes.

Zigzag rocketeers

THICK PAPER, PAINT AND FELT-TIP PENS

1. Cut a strip of thick black paper. Fold up the bottom end, about a third of the way along the strip. Then, fold down the top to meet it.

2. Fold the top of the strip back at the point where the two ends meet. Then, turn the card around so that the bigger section is at the back.

You could add planets or flying saucers to the back section of your card, instead of a rocket.

The shape of your card will depend on the size of the rectangle you cut in step 1.

3. To paint the stars, lay the card on an old newspaper. Dip an old toothbrush into some white paint and spatter it over the card (see page 7).

Draw the helmet on one side of the piece of paper.

4. While the paint is drying, draw a circle for a spaceboy's helmet on a piece of thick white paper. Add a head and face inside.

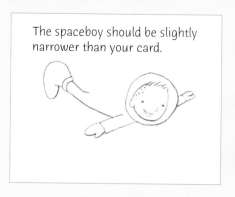

The spaceboy should be slightly narrower than your card.

5. Draw his arms and gloves on either side of the helmet. Then, draw his body and one of his legs. Add a chunky space boot, too.

These three cards had part of a planet glued onto their front sections.

The stripes on some of these planets were drawn with different felt-tip pens.

Leave a white border around your pictures.

Don't spread glue on the top part of the boy or the rocket.

6. Draw the rocket on the spaceboy's back and add a large flame. Draw the other leg and boot, then add flames coming from both boots.

7. Draw a space rocket. Fill in your drawings with paints or felt-tip pens. Then, cut around them when the paint or ink is dry.

8. Fold the black paper into a zizgag again. Glue the rocket on the back section. Then, glue on the spaceboy, below the first fold.

45

Patchwork paper

PATTERNED PAPER FROM OLD MAGAZINES AND COLOURED PAPER

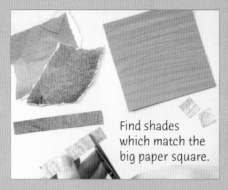

Find shades which match the big paper square.

Don't worry if the pieces don't line up exactly.

1. Cut a square from a piece of thick coloured paper for the front of the card. Then, draw lots of lines across it with a coloured pencil.

2. Cut pieces of patterned paper from old magazines. Cut the pieces into strips, then cut across the strips to make little squares.

3. Glue the patterned pieces onto the square so that it looks like patchwork. Leave spaces between them so that the striped paper shows.

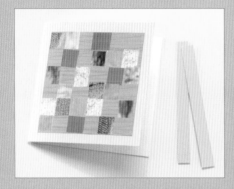

4. Fold a rectangle of thick paper in half for a card. Then, glue the patchwork square onto the front. Trim the edges of the card if you need to.

Add some hearts to the patchwork to make a Valentine's card.

Find out how to make a patchwork heart in 'Other ideas', below.

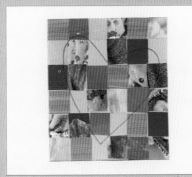

Other ideas

Make a patchwork square by following the steps on the page opposite. Cut it into pieces and glue them onto a card. Add plain shapes, too.

To make a patchwork heart, decorate a square of paper. Then, when the glue is dry, draw a heart on the paper and cut it out.

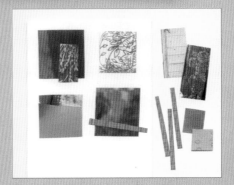

You could decorate a really simple card with squares, rectangles and strips. Cut out the shapes and glue them directly onto a folded card.

Printed animals

THICK CARDBOARD FOR PRINTING, PAINTS AND PENCILS

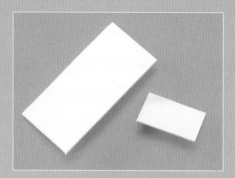

1. Cut a strip of thick cardboard for the dog's body. Then, cut another shorter piece for printing the head, neck, ears and tail.

2. Fold a long rectangle of thick paper in half to make a card. Then, spread some brown paint (acrylic paint works well) onto an old plate.

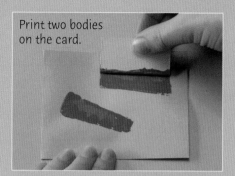

Print two bodies on the card.

3. Drag the edge of the larger piece of cardboard across the paint on the plate. Then, drag the cardboard across the card to print a body.

4. Then, drag the shorter edge of the other smaller piece of cardboard across the paint, and drag it on the paper to print the necks.

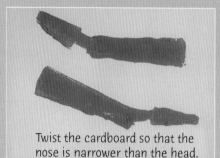

Twist the cardboard so that the nose is narrower than the head.

5. Drag the longer edge of the small piece of cardboard across the paint. Print the heads, twisting the cardboard a little as you drag the paint.

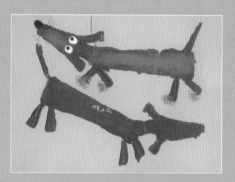

6. Use the cardboard to print the tails and some ears. When the paint is dry, paint eyes and draw collars, noses and claws with pencils.

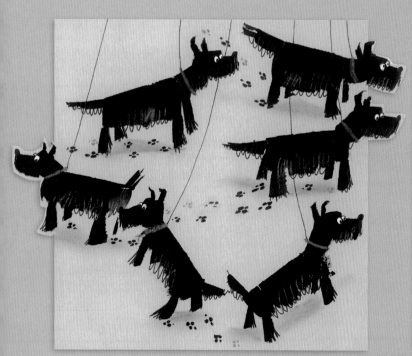

You could draw pawprints and leads, too.

7. Cut around the edges of the card so that the dogs' heads, and tails protrude. Don't cut along the bottom edge though, as the card won't stand up.

This spotty dog card was folded at the top.

Print several lines to make a 'wagging' tail, like the one on the right.

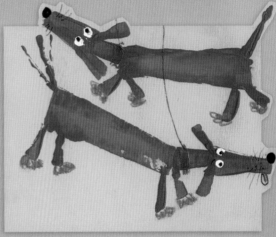

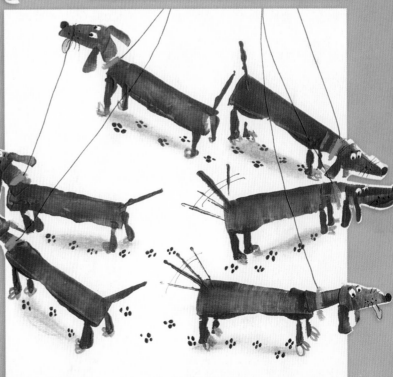

Try printing cats, like these ones.

Dry brush flowers

ACRYLIC PAINT AND THICK PAPER

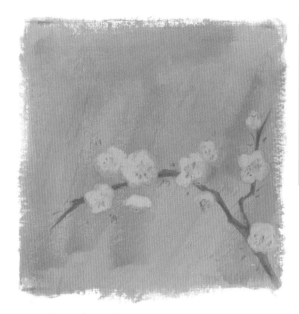

Leave a border around the edge.

Let some of the yellow paint show through.

1. Fold a rectangle of thick paper in half to make a card. Then, dip a dry brush into some yellow paint and paint a square on the card.

2. Before the paint has dried, dip the brush into green paint and roughly dry brush it (see page 7) over part of the yellow square.

You could paint some blossom on a card, too.

Try drawing simple poppy shapes, like the flowers above.

These flowers would be ideal to paint on a Mother's Day card.

Draw the flower faintly.

3. When the paint is dry, draw a shape for the bottom of a flower in the middle of the square. Draw petals, a stem and a leaf, too.

4. Then, fill in the petals using lilac paint on a dry paintbrush. You don't need to follow the pencil lines too closely.

5. Fill in the bottom part of the flower with pink paint on a dry paintbrush. Then, brush one or two faint lines over the petals, too.

Use the ideas shown here to paint different types of flowers.

6. Use a thin paintbrush to paint the stem and the leaf with green paint. Paint a line along the middle of the leaf and add short lines for veins.

Draw faint lines on the petals.

7. When the paint is dry, 'scribble' a pencil line around the edge of the square. Then, draw faint lines on the flower and on the background.

Folded tissue paper

COLOURED PAPER AND TISSUE PAPER

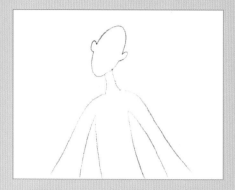

1. Draw an oval head near the top of a piece of white paper. Add ears and a long neck. Then, draw the arms and body, and cut around the shape.

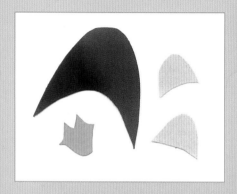

2. For the hat, draw around the head on a piece of black paper. Cut out the shape and add a curved bottom. Cut out lips and eyelids, too.

Instead of drawing a tear shape, you could glue on a sparkly bead, like this one.

3. Glue the hat, eyelids and lips onto the head. Use felt-tip pens to draw the eyebrows, eyes and a black beauty spot. Draw a tear, too.

4. Cut a strip of tissue paper. Fold it in half along its length, so that the fold is at the top. Then, make zigzag pleats all the way along the strip.

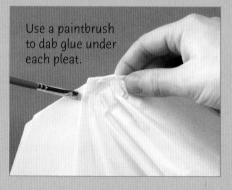

Use a paintbrush to dab glue under each pleat.

5. Spread out the bottom edge of the tissue paper to make a fan shape. Tape the top edge in place, at the back. Then, glue the top of each pleat.

The folded paper could be used for a hat, as well.

Use the same technique to make a ballerina's skirt.

This fan had the edge of a paper doily glued on top of the folded tissue paper.

6. Glue the clown onto a folded card, then glue the pleated collar at the bottom of the neck. Cut out a star and a moon and glue them on, too.

Handbags

SHINY PAPER, THICK PAPER AND BUTTONS

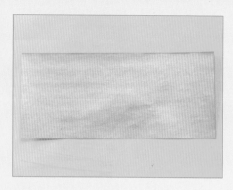

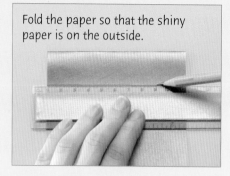

Fold the paper so that the shiny paper is on the outside.

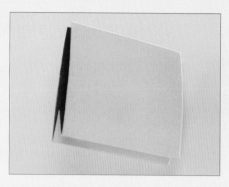

1. Lay a rectangle of shiny paper on a piece of thick paper. Draw around it and cut out the shape. Then, glue the papers together, back to back.

2. Fold the paper in half so that the short edges meet. Then, draw a straight line across the paper, a little way below the fold.

3. Fold the top layer of paper up along the line. Then, turn the paper over and fold up the top side of the paper, matching the fold below.

You could make a suitcase and add a travel tag and labels.

You could make a small purse without handles, like this purple one.

The spots on the bag above were made using a hole puncher.

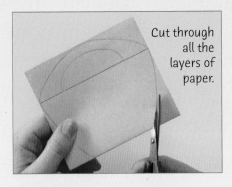

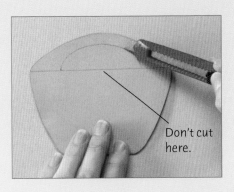

Cut through all the layers of paper.

Don't cut here.

4. Draw the outline of a handbag on the paper. Then, cut around the bag, keeping the paper folded. Don't cut along the bottom, though.

5. Lay the bag on some thick cardboard and use a craft knife to cut around the top curve, only inside the handles, to make a flap.

6. Cut off one of the handles, right across the handbag. Then, fold the flap onto the front and draw a curve around its bottom edge.

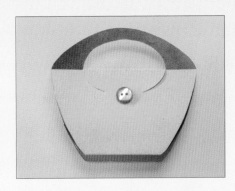

This slit is for securing the flap.

7. Draw another curve, like this. Put some cardboard under the top layer of the bag, then cut along the curve with a craft knife, to make a slit.

8. Remove the cardboard. Then, fold the flap over again and tuck the flap into the slit to secure it. Glue on a button below the slit, too.

Zigzag clowns

THICK PAPER AND PATTERNED PAPER FROM OLD MAGAZINES

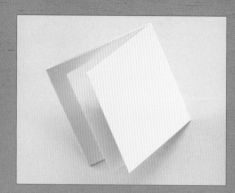 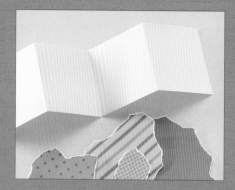 

Snip the tip of the triangle off the body.

1. Cut a long strip from a piece of thick paper. Fold it in half, then in half again. Crease all the folds well, then open out the strip.

2. Fold the card again along the creases, so that it makes a zigzag. Then, cut or rip pieces of patterned paper from old magazines.

3. Cut a triangle of magazine paper for a clown's body. Then, cut more triangular shapes for arms and legs, and glue them onto the card.

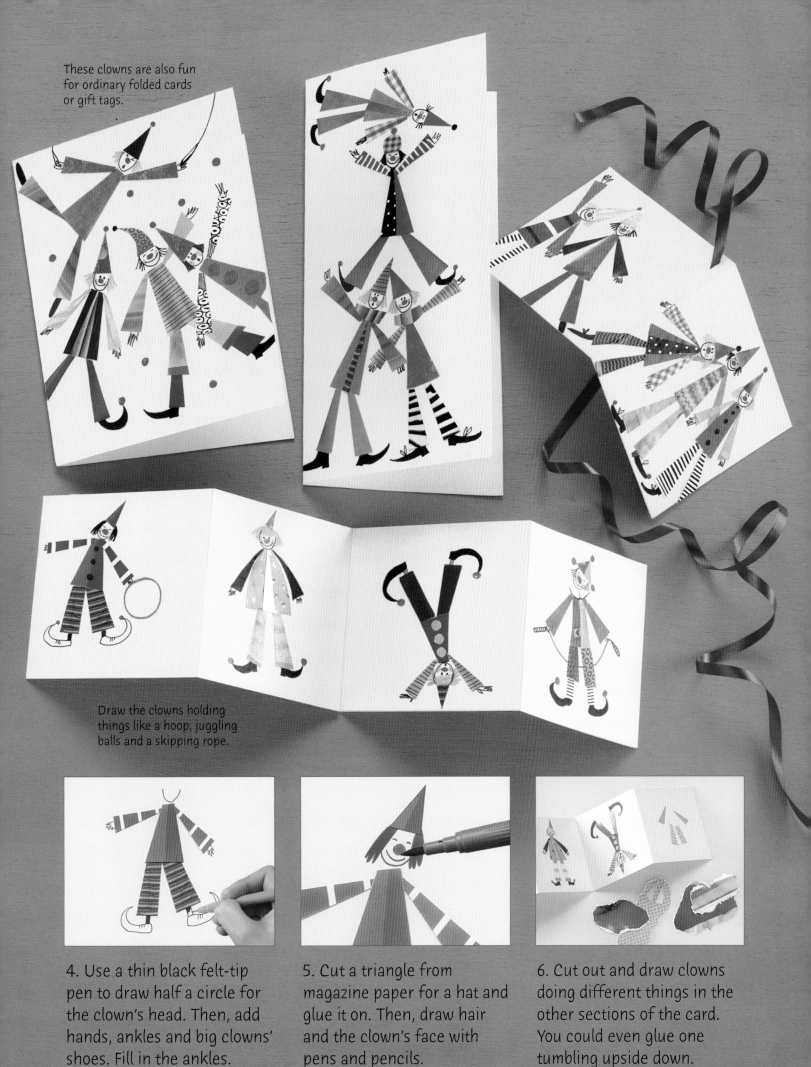

These clowns are also fun for ordinary folded cards or gift tags.

Draw the clowns holding things like a hoop, juggling balls and a skipping rope.

4. Use a thin black felt-tip pen to draw half a circle for the clown's head. Then, add hands, ankles and big clowns' shoes. Fill in the ankles.

5. Cut a triangle from magazine paper for a hat and glue it on. Then, draw hair and the clown's face with pens and pencils.

6. Cut out and draw clowns doing different things in the other sections of the card. You could even glue one tumbling upside down.

Collage animals

THIN CARDBOARD, SCRAPS OF MATERIAL AND BUTTONS

Draw the cat inside the outline of the card.

1. Fold a piece of thin cardboard in half, to make a card. Then, lay the folded card onto a piece of thin paper and draw around it.

2. Draw a half-circle for a cat's body on the paper. Then, add its head and ears. Draw thin legs and a simple curling tail, too.

These cards were made with scraps of felt, thin patterned cotton and denim.

3. Cut out the shape for the cat's head and lay it on a piece of plain material. Hold the paper and draw around it carefully. Cut out the shape.

4. Cut out the shape for the body, then draw around it on some patterned material and cut it out. Do the same for the legs, ears and tail.

5. Glue a piece of ribbon or a strip of material along the bottom of the card. Then, put the shapes of the cat together and glue them on.

This pony had a tiny bead glued on in the middle of the eye.

These cards are easier to make if the shapes of the animals are simple.

6. Cut a strip of material for the stripe on the cat's face and glue it on. Then, either glue on thread for whiskers and a nose, or sew them.

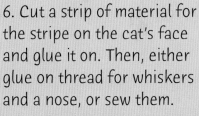

7. Glue on buttons or sequins for eyes. Then, glue another piece of ribbon and more buttons along the bottom of the card.

Making envelopes

THIN PAPER

The cards in this book can be different shapes and sizes. On these pages you can find out how to make two different styles of envelopes to fit the cards you make.

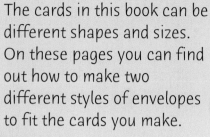

This card was made to fit a bought envelope.

Spread glue up to the fold.

1. For a simple envelope, fold in both long edges of a rectangle of paper. Then, fold up the bottom of the paper, like this.

2. Unfold the paper and spread glue along the folded-in edges. Fold the bottom of up again and rub your fingers along the edges.

The flowery envelopes below were made with wrapping paper.

Pink paper was glued onto the back of blue paper to make this simple envelope.

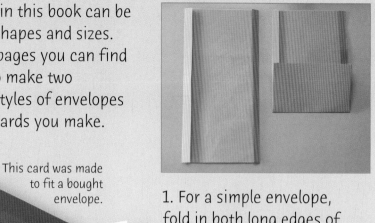

This pink envelope was made with embossed paper (see pages 42-43).

This envelope was made with sponged paper (see page 7).

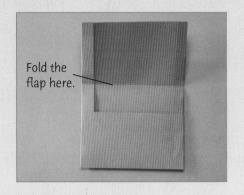

Fold the flap here.

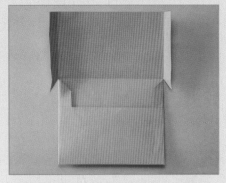

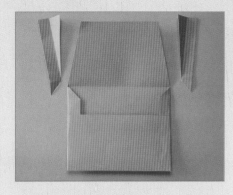

3. Fold the paper over to make the top flap of the envelope, but don't fold it right down against the bottom flap.

4. Unfold the top flap, then make a diagonal cut into one of the folded-in edges. Do the same to the other edge, then fold out the egdes.

5. Cut off the sides of the top flap to make slanted edges. You will need to secure the flap with sticky tape when your card is inside.

Square envelopes

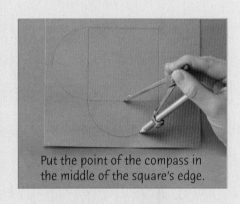

Put the point of the compass in the middle of the square's edge.

1. Lay a square card in the middle of a piece of paper and draw around it. Then, mark the middle point on each side of the square.

2. Use a pencil and a pair of compasses to draw semicircular shapes for flaps on each side of the square. Then, cut around the flaps.

Thick wrapping paper, like this blue paper, is good for making envelopes.

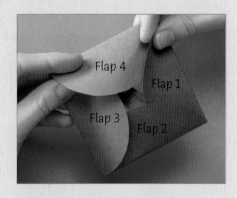

Flap 4
Flap 1
Flap 3
Flap 2

3. Fold flap 1 into the middle of the card, followed by flap 2, then flap 3. Then, tuck flap 4 under flap 1 to hold the other flaps in place.

Other ideas

These pages show you more ideas for making cards, using techniques from earlier in this book. Turn back to the pages which are mentioned to find out how they were done.

This sunset card was made using strips of paper (see pages 30-31).

Instead of drawing clothes, like the dress on page 28, cut them from paper instead.

A dry brushed snowman (see pages 50-51).

The car card below uses the same technique as the bugs on pages 26-27.

The houses below are collages made from textured paper (see pages 6-7).

This Christmas card uses the technique on pages 18-19.

The dragon above also uses the technique shown on pages 18-19.

For glittery Easter eggs, see pages 38-39.

This butterfly card is made with scraps of paper from old magazines (see pages 56-57).

This hearts card would make an ideal Valentine's Day card (see pages 34-35).

Use folded tissue paper for a bird's tail (see pages 52-53).

This collage doll card is made like the animals on pages 58-59.

Index

animals,
  black and white, 18-19,
    62, 63
  collage, 58-59
  printed, 48-49
  stand-up, 12-13

birds, textured, 24-25
bugs, ink, 26-27

collage,
  material,
    collage animals,
      58-59, 63
    stitched flowers,
      34-35, 63
  paper,
    folded tissue paper,
      52-53, 63
    patchwork paper, 46-47
    stand-up animals, 12-13
    striped patterns,
      30-31, 62
    textured birds, 6, 24-25
    wrapping paper kites,
      32-33
    zigzag clowns, 56-57, 63
coloured pencil drawing,
  birthday cakes, 14-15
  ink bugs, 26-27, 62
  stylish shoes, 10-11

dry brushing,
  different papers, 6-7
  dry brush flowers, 50-51
  swirly flowers, 6, 8-9
  wrapping paper kites,
    32-33

embossing,
  embossed cards, 42-43
  envelopes, 60
envelopes, 5
  making, 60-61
fold-out cards, 36-37
flowers,
  dry brush, 50-51
  stitched, 34-35
  swirly, 6, 8-9

magazine paper,
  different papers, 6-7
  zigzag clowns, 56-57, 63
  patchwork paper, 46-47
material,
  collage animals, 58-59, 63
  other ideas, 63
  stitched flowers, 34-35
materials, 4-5

painted cards,
  dry brush flowers, 50-51
  printed animals, 48-49
  swirly flowers, 8-9
  watercolour leaves, 40-41
patterned cards,
  glittery patterns, 38-39, 63
  silver swirls, 22-23
  striped patterns, 30-31, 62
pen drawings,
  birthday cakes, 14-15
  black and white animals,
    20-21, 62, 63
  decorated drawings, 28-29, 62
  ink bugs, 26-27, 62
  stylish shoes, 10-11
  zigzag clowns, 56-57

pop-up cards,
  fold-out cards, 36-37
  pop-up buildings, 16-17
  rocket launch, 20-21

spattering,
  different papers, 6-7
  zigzag rocketeers, 44-45
sponging
  different papers, 6-7
  envelopes, 60-61

textured paper
  different papers, 6-7
  glittery patterns, 38-39
  textured birds, 6, 24-25
  wrapping paper kites,
    32-33
3-D cards,
  fold-out cards, 36-37
  handbags, 54-55
  pop-up buildings, 16-17
  rocket launch, 20-21
  stand-up animals, 12-13
  swirly flowers, 6, 8-9
  watercolour leaves, 40-41
  zigzag rocketeers, 44-45

wrapping paper,
  different papers, 6-7
  wrapping paper kites,
    32-33
  envelopes, 60-61

zigzag cards,
  watercolour leaves, 40-41
  zigzag clowns, 56-57, 63
  zigzag rocketeers, 44-45